The Scrimshaw Ring

For information about permission to reproduce selections from this book, write to

PERMISSIONS
THE VERMONT FOLKLIFE CENTER
MASONIC HALL
3 COURT STREET, BOX 442
MIDDLEBURY, VERMONT 05753

LIBRARY OF CONGRESS | CATALOGING-IN-PUBLICATION DATA

Jaspersohn, William.
    The scrimshaw ring / by William Jaspersohn ; illustrations by Vernon Thornblad.— 1st ed.
        p. cm. — (The family heritage series)
    Based on real events.
    Summary: A young boy living in Newport, Rhode Island, in 1710 enjoys imaginary adventures
with make-believe pirates, until the day that real pirates come ashore for evil purposes and leave
him a remarkable memento. Includes ideas for activities related to
family heirlooms.
    ISBN 0-916718-19-0 (hardcover)
    [1. Pirates—Fiction. 2. Heirlooms—Fiction. 3. Newport (R.I.)—History—Colonial period,
ca. 1600-1775—Fiction.] I. Thornblad, Vernon, ill. II. Title. III. Series.

PZ7.J323 Sc 2002
[Fic]—dc21

                                                                                    2002004314

ISBN 0-916718-19-0
Printed in Hong Kong
Distributed by Independent Publishers Group (IPG)
814 North Franklin Street, Chicago, IL 60610

First Edition

Book design: Joseph Lee, Black Fish Design
Series Editor: William Jaspersohn

10 9 8 7 6 5 4 3 2 1

Publication of this book was made possible by grants from the Acadia Fund, Inc.,
and the Christian A. Johnson Endeavor Foundation.

A FAMILY HERITAGE BOOK

from the

VERMONT FOLKLIFE

CENTER

The Scrimshaw Ring

BY WILLIAM JASPERSOHN

PAINTINGS BY VERNON THORNBLAD

Once, long ago, on a farm
by the sea, there lived a kindly couple
and their young son, William.

William was a happy, imaginative boy. To him, his parents' farm was a peaceable kingdom, a beautiful paradise framed by the sparkling sea.

When William was six, his father gave him a knife. With it, William whittled a fish pole, a reed pipe and a cutlass. When he bobbed for mackerel in the shallows down by the cove, he pretended the fish were whales and sea serpents. When he played his reed pipe for the bobolinks in the marsh, he pretended the notes cast a spell on them. And when he ran through the woods and fields behind the house, and swung his wooden cutlass down on the beach, he pretended he was battling pirates.

He had never seen a pirate in his life, but that did not stop him from spinning stories about them. Often, he told his parents the stories at bedtime. "Yes, yes." His father would pat him on the head. "Very nice, very nice. Go to sleep now."

The cook called William "a fanciful boy." His parents called him "our little Tale-Teller."

One foggy dawn, William's father shook
him awake and said, "William, your mother
and I are going into town on errands. We shall
be gone all day, and while we are away, I want
you to stay near the house and keep Cook
company. Is that clear?"

"Yes, father."

With that, his parents kissed him goodbye
and departed by buggy, disappearing up the
lane into the cool, gray fog.

All that morning, William stayed indoors, whittling and helping the cook with the housekeeping. At noon, as the fog lifted, the cook went out to the garden to pick some vegetables for lunch. When she looked down on the cove, she screamed and ran away.

William heard the scream and rushed to the window.

There, in the cove, he saw a small ship at anchor.

It flew no flag and showed no signs of life, but rowing toward shore was a longboat filled with men.

They were rough, wild, fearsome men with filthy hair, faded clothes, curved pistols and sharp cutlasses. Some wore scuffed shoes with holes in their soles and woolen coats with pewter buttons. Others were barefoot with knobbed toes and thick yellow toenails. Some wore their hair pulled back in a pigtail dabbed with tar and knotted with a grimy ribbon. Others had long ago shaved their heads to rid their scalps of lice and fleas.

In the boat, wrapped in a piece of canvas, was the body of a dead man, the first mate. Bound with ropes from head to toe was an angry man, the ship's captain.

William had no way of knowing it, but these men were mutineers. They had seized control of the ship from the captain because he was cruel, mean and unfair to them. They liked the first mate because he'd taken their side when they'd mutinied.

The captain had fired his pistol as they rushed him and shot the first mate dead. That was the last shot the captain would ever fire.

From his place at the kitchen window, William could see what the men were doing, but he could not see very well. That was a good thing. For, on a sunken road above the beach, the men from the ship dug two deep holes. In one, they placed the body of the first mate. In the other, they would place the captain. But first, with gun or cutlass (to this day, no one knows which), they took their revenge and killed him.

When this terrible deed was done and the bodies were buried, the men placed a small white stone at the head and foot of each grave. Then they tramped up into the barnyard, captured the chickens, ducks and geese, and drove all the sheep, hogs and cattle down to the beach.

As they marched past the house with the livestock, William peeked up from the window. Big mistake! A mutineer saw him. William ducked down, but it was too late! "I am sunk now," he thought.

With cutlass drawn, the mutineer entered the house. He was dark and small, with bright, weaselly eyes, and gave off a stink of bilgewater and sweat. He saw William huddled in the corner. William could hardly breathe. "I am going to be stabbed," he thought. "I am going to die."

Instead, seeing it was only a boy, the
mutineer did something remarkable. With
the flat of his cutlass, he touched William
on the shoulder. William opened his
eyes. Bending close, the mutineer slid
a ring off his finger and placed it
in William's trembling hand.
William looked at him. The
mutineer smiled. Without
a word, he patted William
on the cheek, nodded
once, then rushed from
the house to join his
shipmates. Within an
hour, the pirates had
sailed off.

Late that afternoon, when William's parents
returned home, they were shocked to discover the
cook gone and the barn empty.

"What happened?" they asked. "Where are the
animals?"

William told them everything, but his father only
frowned.

"William!" he snapped. "Is this one of your stories?"

"No, sir. No, it's not."

He showed his parents the gravesite. Then he
showed them the ring. It was big and square and
carved from a single piece of whalebone—scrimshaw.
His father studied it for a long, long time.

"Pirates," he muttered, and hugged his son. And
hugged him. And hugged him. And hugged him.

For a time after that, William would not
venture far from the house. But no other
pirates ever came up to it, and after a while
William regained his old confidence. "The
world is a beautiful place," he thought.
"But, in truth, sometimes it is dangerous."

As for the ring, William kept it, and many years later passed it on to his firstborn son. And many years after that, the son passed it on to his first child. And so on, as families do, through seven generations.

One day, nearly three hundred years after it happened, an old man told the pirate story, just as he had heard it, to his grandson. When it was over, the boy asked if the story was really true.

"Open your hand," was all the grandfather said.

In it, he placed the pirate's scrimshaw ring.

ABOUT THIS TALE

The Scrimshaw Ring is based on real events that occurred in Newport, Rhode Island, around the year 1710. A boy named William (last name, Bateman) really did live with his parents on a big coastal farm there, and pirates really did come ashore and do everything described in the story, including giving William a hand-carved scrimshaw ring inlaid with the portrait of a Spanish lady. Believed to be the oldest piece of inlaid scrimshaw on record, the ring was passed down through generations of Batemans and Becks until, sadly, in the 1990s, it was lost. Horace Beck, a renowned folklorist and descendant of William Bateman, first heard the story of the scrimshaw ring from his grandparents, who lived in the Bateman house through the 1920s. "I spent my weekends and summers at that house," Horace remembers. "By then, the house was bigger, but the white stones that marked the pirate graves were still there. As for the ring, its hole was so small, I couldn't even put it on my little finger!"

An heirloom is an object passed down in a family through many generations because the object is treasured by family members. Heirlooms can be anything: photographs of family members or important family places, artwork, furniture, diaries, letters, maps, tools, jewelry, silverware, dishes, clothing, toys, quilts, holiday ornaments—even a favorite family recipe.

Often, heirlooms are the source of wonderful stories and narratives. *The Scrimshaw Ring* is an example of an heirloom story that was passed down through seven generations of the Bateman and Beck families.

Why not see what heirloom stories *your* family has?

Heirlooms

Go to older family members—parents, grandparents, aunts, uncles—and ask them to show you their important family heirlooms. Maybe the heirloom is a picture of a family member who is no longer alive. Maybe it's a family antique, such as a painting, a chair, a watch, a dish, a dress.

Have the older person tell you all about the heirloom and why it is important to your family. Maybe there is a story connected to the heirloom and the family members who used it. With the help of your family, write down the story about the heirloom so that it's never forgotten.

Choose an object important to you and make it an instant heirloom. Is there a toy or some other object of yours that you might wish to pass on to your children someday? If so, cherish that object; write about it so that you can give your children that writing too.

Sponsor a Family Heirloom Day at your school. On that day, have everybody in your class bring in family heirlooms and share stories about them. Try it. Heirlooms are great touchstones to the past!